JUNA AND APPA

by Jane Park

illustrated by Felicia Hoshino

Lee & Low Books Inc. New York

LEE & LOW BOOKS Inc., 95 Madison Avenue, New York, NY 10016
leeandlow.com
Edited by Jessica V. Echeverria
Designed by David and Susan Neuhaus/NeuStudio
Production by The Kids at Our House
The text is set in Cotoris
The illustrations are rendered in watercolor

Manufactured in China by RR Donnelley
10 9 8 7 6 5 4 3 2 1
First Edition

Library of Congress Cataloging-in-Publication Data
Names: Bahk, Jane, author. | Hoshino, Felicia, illustrator.
Title: Juna and Appa / by Jane Bahk; illustrated by Felicia Hoshino.
Description: First edition. | New York: Lee & Low Books Inc., [2022]
Audience: Ages 4-8. | Audience: Grades 2-3. | Summary: "A young Korean American girl enjoys
helping her father in their dry cleaning shop, but when a customer berates her father for losing a jacket,
Juna goes on a magical quest to help her father recover what is lost"—Provided by publisher.
Identifiers: LCCN 2021016333 | ISBN 9781643792279 (hardcover) | ISBN 9781643795287 (ebk)
Subjects: CYAC: Fathers and daughters—Fiction. | Imagination—Fiction.
Lost and found possessions—Fiction. | Dry cleaning industry—Fiction.
Animals—Habits and behavior—Fiction. | Korean Americans—Fiction.
Classification: LCC PZ7.B14225 Js 2022 | DDC [E]—dc23
LC record available at https://lccn.loc.gov/2021016333

FSC
www.fsc.org
MIX
Paper from
responsible sources
FSC® C144853

For Appa 아빠 and Umma 엄마.
And always, Ena and Keo —J.

For Dad. Love, F.

Juna's favorite day of the week was Saturday.
   That's when she helped her father at their
dry cleaning shop.
   She'd find customers' clothes and sort
spools of thread by color.
   Appa called her his little helper, even
when she made mistakes.

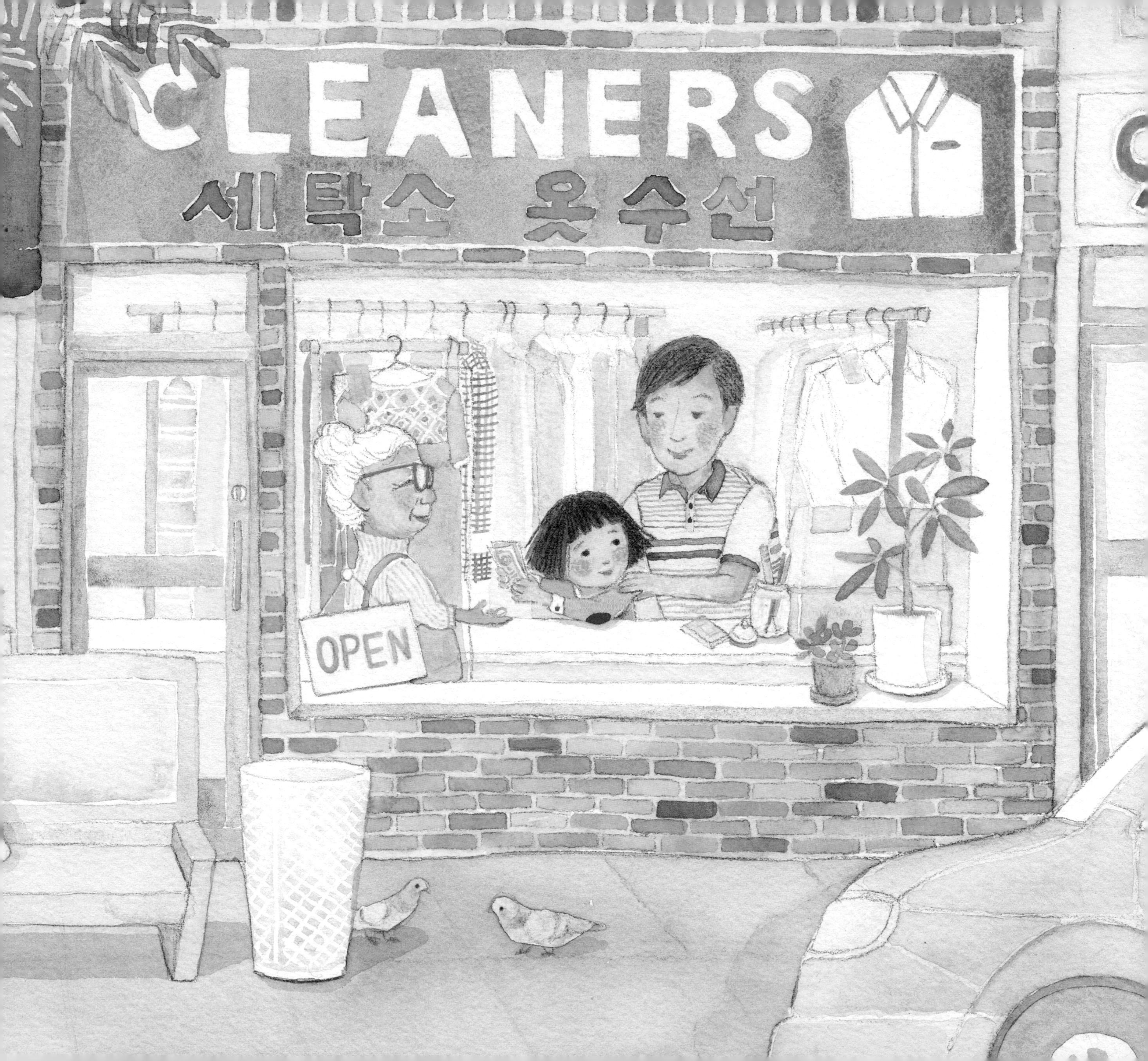
CLEANERS
세탁소 옷수선
OPEN

The best part was at the end of the day when Juna turned the sign to Closed, and she and Appa walked to the taco truck parked across the street.

They always ordered five carne asada tacos.
"Ahh, masitda! So delicious!" Appa would say after his first bite.

But one Saturday while Juna was stamping
bags, she heard Mr. Parker shouting at Appa.
   Appa could not find Mr. Parker's very
expensive jacket with gold buttons.
The jacket was lost.
Juna had never seen Appa look so worried.

"Appa, I can help find it!"
Juna said after Mr. Parker left.

"Juna, please just sit still,"
Appa said. "That will help."

Juna tried to sit still.

She thought about how nice Appa would look in a fancy jacket.

Maybe she could buy him one for his birthday with her New Year money.

A puff of steam from the pants presser warmed her face and wrapped around her as she closed her eyes.

Juna walked through a foggy field.

She stumbled into a grassy pit and found herself surrounded by large eggs.

A giant appa rhea bird peered down at her.

"Have you seen a fancy jacket with gold buttons?" Juna asked.

"Oh, are you cold? I'll warm you up!" said the appa bird, and covered her with some leaves and grass.

Juna nestled in with his eggs.
The big bird hummed a song that Appa always whistled.
But the bird's beak felt sharp and cold when it nuzzled her
face. It was not like Appa's warm nose.

Juna looked for Appa to hum the song to him.
She hoped he would whistle along.

Instead, he said, "Juna, please sit quietly."

Juna tried to sit quietly.

She helped put cardboard strips onto wire hangers.

Perfect for a fishing pole, Juna thought.

She tied some thread onto a strip and used a paper clip for a hook.

She threw the line into the giant laundry basket.

Juna felt a tug on the line.

She tugged back.

A strong jerk pulled Juna inside the basket and down into a dark pond.

When she surfaced, Juna bumped into a water bug.

"Are you looking for something?" the appa water bug asked.

"I'm looking for a fancy jacket with gold buttons," Juna said. "Have you seen it?"

"The only jackets here are yellowjackets." The appa water bug laughed. "Hop on and I'll take you somewhere safer."

"But your back is covered with bumps!" Juna said.

"They're my eggs," the appa water bug said. "Don't worry. They won't fall off."

Juna held on tight.

She remembered when she'd lost a shoe at the park and Appa had carried her to the car.

With Appa's piggybacks, Juna always felt safe.

Juna climbed on Appa's back.
"Uhbuhjo, uhbuhjo," she said, wanting a piggyback.
Appa fell backward.

"Juna, please!" he said. "Gamani-issuh!"
Juna's eyes burned with tears.
Maybe Appa would like it better if she weren't there at all.

Juna ran down the rows of plastic-covered clothes until she reached a forest.

By a river, Juna met a Darwin's frog with a jiggly belly.

"Have you seen a very fancy jacket with gold buttons?"
Juna asked the appa frog.

"*Croak, croak!*" said the Darwin's frog.

"I'm sorry, I don't understand," Juna said.

"*CROAK, CROAK!*"

"Shouting never helps anyone understand better,"
Juna said.

"*CROOOOOAAAK!!!*"

The Darwin's frog opened its mouth and out jumped tiny frogs, one after the other.

"Good-bye! Good luck!" he called out to the tiny frogs.

"Good-bye?" repeated Juna. "But they're so small! How do they know what to do?"

"I've kept them safe, and they've learned what to do from watching me," said the appa frog. "Parents show love in lots of different ways."

"Juna-ya!" she heard Appa call. "Where are you?"

Juna stood up and ran toward Appa's voice.

Juna popped out from beneath a pile of clothes.
"There you are!" Appa said. "You made me worry!"

"About me?" Juna asked. "Appa, will finding Mr. Parker's jacket make everything better?"

"Maybe not everything." Appa sighed. "But my mistake could cost us a lot."

"You always say everyone makes mistakes," Juna said. "I have my New Year money saved. You can give it to Mr. Parker."

Appa looked at Juna.

"Always my hardworking helper," he said.

"I will look for the jacket on Monday," Appa said, standing up tall. "And you will keep your money. Are you hungry?"

Juna felt warmer than lying in a rhea's nest.

Safer than riding on a water bug's back.

And more fearless than a Darwin's frog.

Juna smiled and turned the sign to Closed.
She slipped her hand into Appa's, and they
walked to the taco truck parked across the street.

JUNA MEETS SOME OF THE MOST INTERESTING DADS IN THE ANIMAL KINGDOM.

GREATER RHEA

The greater rhea lives in South America and is one of the largest birds in the world—standing at three to five feet tall. The male rhea builds a nest in the ground where the female rhea lays eggs. Then the male takes over and sits on up to fifty eggs for six weeks. After they hatch, the male raises the dozens of chicks alone.

GIANT WATER BUG

Many insects lay their eggs under a leaf or rock, but the female giant water bug lays them on a moving object: the male's wings! Unable to fly, he carries the eggs around, safe from predators, until they hatch.

DARWIN'S FROG

Also known as **sapito vaquero** (cowboy frog) for its distinctive call, the Darwin's frog lives in cool forests of Chile and Argentina. After its eggs hatch, the male frog will swallow his tadpoles to keep them safe in his vocal sac. When the time is right, he'll "burp" up full-grown frogs.

AUTHOR'S NOTE

Growing up, I spent a lot of time at my parents' dry-cleaning shop after school. My parents talk about these challenging times with some sadness, but I remember having a lot of fun. The shop was a magical place with the most amazing business supplies. My hope is that this book provides a mirror for the many kids growing up in their family's shops. For others, it may be a window to get to know the people working behind the shop counters and their kids, who also see their parents as their heroes.